**For John-Patrick and Cormac, and for everyone
who wants to befriend a fish —NM**

**For my children: Roisin, Sheila, Aine,
and baby Denny —JAF**

To Alexis —MS

Dial Books for Young Readers
An imprint of Penguin Random House LLC, New York

First published in the United States of America by Dial Books for Young Readers,
an imprint of Penguin Random House LLC, 2022

Visit us online at penguinrandomhouse.com.

Library of Congress Cataloging-in-Publication Data is available.

Manufactured in China • TOPL • ISBN 9780593324752 • 10 9 8 7 6 5 4 3 2 1

Design by Mina Chung • Text set in Mikado Medium

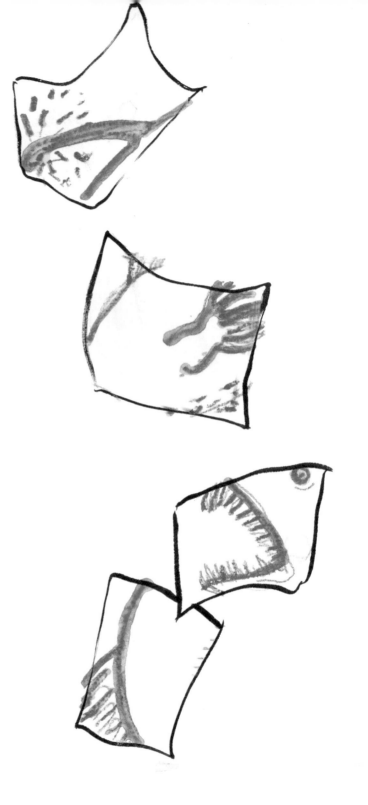

ATHA MAY and the ANGLER FISH

Nora Morrison and Jessie Ann Foley

illustrated by Mika Song

Dial Books
for Young Readers

One rainy morning
in science room ten,
Mrs. Marino cried:
"Pick up your pens!

"Children," she said,
"we have spent the last week
exploring the world
of the wet salty deep!

"The Arctic! The Pacific!
The Atlantic wild way!
The—are you chewing gum,
Miss Agatha May?

"Each of you scholars
will research a creature
that lives in the ocean.
You'll learn all its features:

"its scales or its claws,
its suckers or stingers,
its—what is that mess all over your fingers?

"Pick any sea-dweller
from under the sun,
but no two children
may choose the same one!

"Many fish in the sea,
from South to North Pole,
and—what is that smell?
Cod casserole?

"Agatha May,
you must pay attention,
unless you'd prefer to
wind up in detention?"

"Next comes Lavinia, Leandra, and Li,
then Tina and Gina and Courtney McGee."

As Agatha listened, the tears gathered fast.
She had NO merit points! Her turn would be last!
She was tardy and dreamy, her interests were odd,
her fingers were charcoaled, her breath smelled like cod!

Another girl surely would steal her choice first.
Oh, Mrs. Marino was simply the worst!

So she sat in sad silence while girls picked their topics:
crustaceans, cetaceans from arctic to tropics.
The **narwhal** was chosen, the **walrus** and **whale**,
anemones, manatees, sharks of all tails.

The **Socotran snakelet** from the waters of Yemen,
the **Dungeness crab** that tastes so good with lemon.
Next went the **dolphin**, with all its charms,
and lastly the **octopus**, with all its arms.

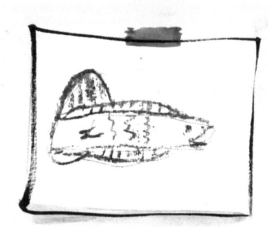

But then something happened!
Something **wondrous** and **strange**!
It was Agatha's turn—
and her **fish** was **unclaimed**!

Could it be a mistake?
A strange sort of error?
They'd left out the **ANGLER,**
that **glorious terror**!

Each student was ready
to present that Monday
though perhaps none so ready
as **Agatha May**—

when she heard her name called,
she threw down her pen
and dashed to the front
of science room ten.

"There's a zone in the ocean called the bathypelagic,
a mysterious place so murky and magic
that no human eye has plumbed its black gloom—
it's more unexplored than even the moon!

"And in this strange place,
four thousand feet under,
the anglerfish prowls,
a **pelagic wonder!**

"Humans don't **hunt** it.
Humans don't **eat** it.
Humans can't **touch** it.
Humans can't **reach** it!

"It's not in a fish tank,
or even a zoo,
you'd not want to pet it—
it's covered with **goo!**

"This ambushing fish
of the **deep-deep-sea** zone
has no **fins** and no **skin**—
it barely has **bones**!

"It swallows prey **whole**!
It has teeth sharp as **pins**!
And perhaps most astonishing:
It can't even **swim**!

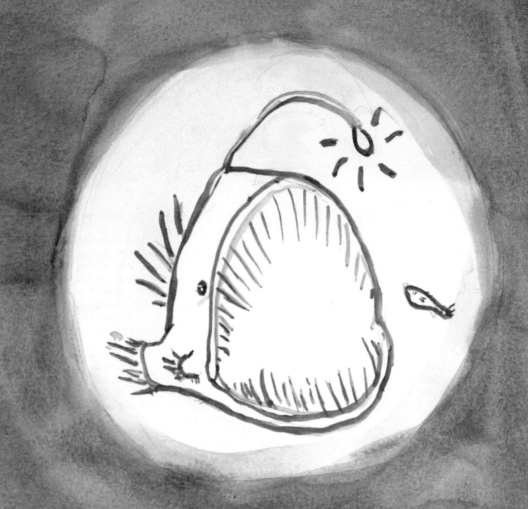

"It wobbles around,
Waving its lure—
a glowing blue speck
in a darkness so pure

"that when curious fish
come to check out this light,
it swallows them whole
in one massive bite!"

"Did you say it lights up?"
"**Indeed!** See, in essence,
it glows through a process called
bioluminescence!"

"**But how does it glow?**"
asked Amaya Ophelia.
"Using **proteins**," cried Agatha,
"in its **bacteria!**"

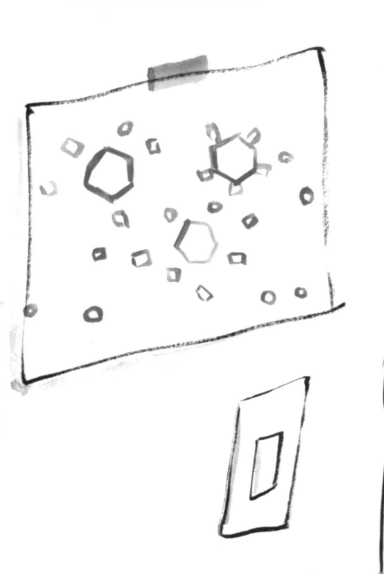

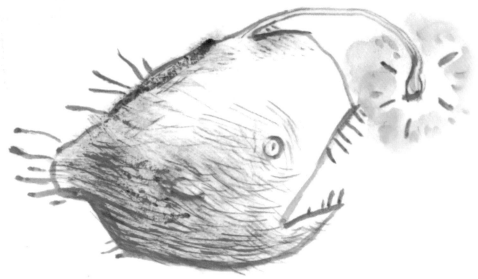

"Sorry, did you say a fishing pole?"
asked Leandra Francesca.
"Well, the technical term is a
'**bulbous esca**.'"

"But where does it glow?"
asked Lavinia Stead.
"From a **fishing pole** fused to the
front of its head!"

"Now let me continue!
Please don't interrupt!
When anglerfish mate,
their bodies get stuck!"

"It looks like a monster!"

"It looks like a gorgon!"

"After they mate,
the male loses his organs!"

"This fish is amazing!"

"This fish is horrific!"

"This fish is astounding!"

"This fish is terrific!"

"Miss Agatha May,
 please stay after class."
"I'll be late for mathematics—"
"I'll give you a pass."

Was the problem her questions?
The mess of her desk?
The F that she got
on her last science test?

She was in deep-sea trouble,
and now she must pay,
for teachers are creatures
who ambush their prey!

"Agatha May! I am highly impressed—
For your presentation was simply the best!"

Better than Lavinia's, Leandra's, or Li's?
Or Tina's or Gina's or Courtney McGee's?
Better than Joyce, Amaya, or Jen?
Better than MARY LOU, queen of room ten?

"Your desk is a mess,
and your cubby a fright,
but your mind is a treasure.
It pulsates with light.

"And one of these days,
an explorer will reach
the faraway bottom
of the wet salty deep.

"And that's why, my dear scholar,
I pester you so:
to push you to places
you know you must go."

And Agatha May could do nothing but nod—
for although she was messy and tardy and odd,
a dream had now hatched in the sea of her heart,
and when dreams begin swimming, well—

that's the **best** part.

AGATHA MAY'S ANGLERFISH FILES

ANGLERFISH FACTS

- There are more than 200 species of anglerfish in the ocean. They can be grouped into four categories: batfish, goosefish, frogfish, and deep-sea anglers!

- Anglerfish live in every ocean in the world!

- Only female anglerfish have lures. They lure prey with a "fishing rod" tipped with glowing bacteria that live in symbiosis with the fish.

- Anglerfish are poor swimmers. They can paddle in bursts but can't easily swim like most fish.

- Anglerfish don't hunt—instead, they have lures to bring food to them and huge mouths to help them eat it fast. This is why we call them "ambush predators."

- Because anglerfish are flexible and have huge mouths, they can swallow prey that is twice their size!

- For most anglerfish, when a male finds a female, he bites her skin and attaches himself to her so he's guaranteed to have a mate. He's much smaller than her! Then he matures into an adult . . . and loses most of his organs. He is literally a parasite and steals her nutrients. Up to eight males may fuse to one female in some species.

LIGHT AND DARKNESS

Bioluminescence is used by 70 percent of species in the Mesopelagic zone, but it becomes less common in more shallow and deeper waters. Bioluminescence can help animals conceal their shape and lure prey—or stun it!

It's dark down there. By 33 feet, 84 percent of light from the surface is gone. By 330 feet, 99 percent of light is filtered out. And the color changes. Red light is filtered out in the shallows, then orange and yellow and green. Eventually everything looks blue. Then black.